Aa is for Arctic

Global warming is melting the ice!

The Sun warms the Earth near the Equator

Antarctica is the coldest place on Earth

and Antarctica

Bb   is for Biodiversity

AMPHIBIAN	BUTTERFLY	CAT	DOG	ELEPHANT
FLOWERS	GULL	HUMAN	INSECT	JELLYFISH
KANGAROO	LION	MONKEY	NEWT	OWL
PIG	QUEENBEE	RABBIT	SNAKE	TORTOISE
UNICORN MYTH	VULTURE	WHALE	eXtinct	ZEBRA

Yellow bird

BIODIVERSITY IS THE VARIETY OF LIFE ON EARTH

Cc is for Coral Reef

Ancient habitat living under the sea
Tiny organisms form a colony of
limestone which absorbs carbon

Dd is for Desert

Life struggles to survive in this dry land with little rainfall. The camel stores water in its hump.

Ee is for Ecosystem

Bees are vital for biodiversity
pollinating flowers, fruit and crops.

Ff is for Fossil Fuels

Coal, oil and gas are the decayed remains of prehistoric life extracted from deep underground.

Gg is for Greenhouse Gases

Burning fossil fuels releases carbon dioxide into the atmosphere which traps the heat like a greenhouse.

Hh is for Habitat

Places providing food and shelter necessary for Nature.

Ii is for Insects

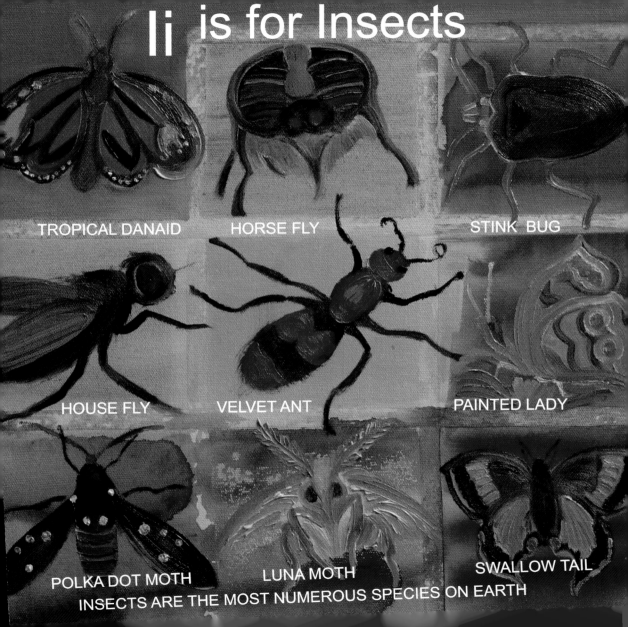

TROPICAL DANAID

HORSE FLY

STINK BUG

HOUSE FLY

VELVET ANT

PAINTED LADY

POLKA DOT MOTH

LUNA MOTH

SWALLOW TAIL

INSECTS ARE THE MOST NUMEROUS SPECIES ON EARTH

Jj is for Jungle

Don't get lost!

Kk is for Knowledge.
We have enough
to
save our Planet!

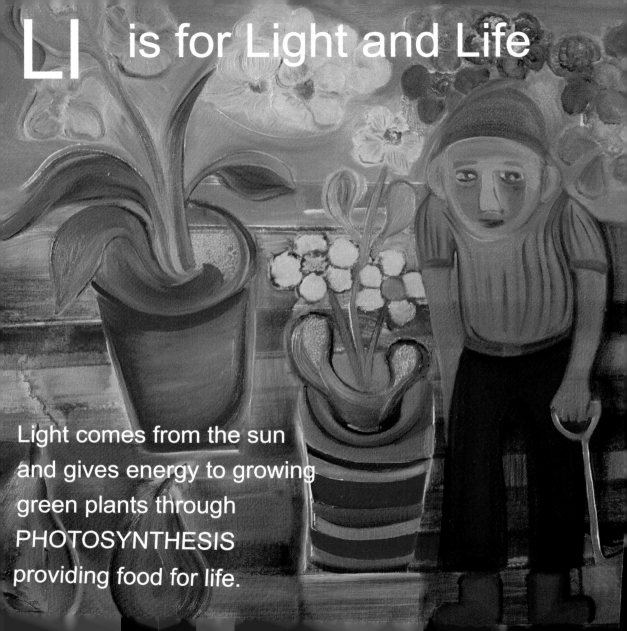

Ll is for Light and Life

Light comes from the sun
and gives energy to growing
green plants through
PHOTOSYNTHESIS
providing food for life.

Mm is for Marine Life

Marine life is threatened by warmer seas, over fishing and pollutants such as plastic.

Nn is for Natural Resources

Solar Panels absorb heat from the sun converting it into electricity and wind turns the Turbine Blades

Oo is for Oceans

ARCTIC OCEAN

NORTH ATLANTIC OCEAN

PACIFIC OCEAN

PACIFIC OCEAN

SOUTH ATLANTIC OCEAN

INDIAN OCEAN

ANTARCTIC OCEAN

The five Oceans cover over two thirds of the Planet and make up our largest Ecosystem.

Pp is for Photosynthesis

Plants use energy from the sun to convert carbon dioxide into oxygen and sugars. Water is taken up by the roots.

Qq is for Quotas

Quotas are the amount of goods, such as fish, which a country is allowed to import or export.

Rr is for Rainforest

Tropical Rainforests near the Equator are hot and wet containing a great variety of plant and animal life.

Ss is for Sustainability

Sustainability is about taking care of our Planet and not using up Earth's valuable resources.

"Would you like a veggie sausage?"

Tt is for Trees

Trees can live for hundreds of years but can be cut down in a day reducing the amount of oxygen being recycled into the atmosphere.

Uu is for Urbanization

Human populations have spread out over the Planet, moving from rural areas to look for work in the cities, encroaching on Natural Habitats.

Vv is for Volcanoes

Volcanoes are powerful natural phenomena through which lava, gas and ash are ejected through an opening in the earth's crust.

Ww   is for Weather

Global warming is causing more extreme weather leading to floods, fires and drought.

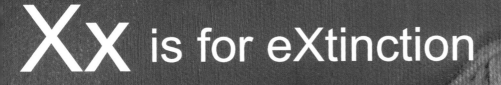

Xx is for eXtinction

We will go the way of the dinosaurs
if we do not achieve our targets.

Yy is for Young People

Our Future!

Zz is for

Zero

emissions

by 2050